Ten Little Dinosaurs

Written by Pattie L. Schnetzler

Illustrated by Jim Harris

ACCORD PUBLISHING
a division of Andrews McMeel Publishing, LLC
Kansas City, Missouri

 Ten little dinosaurs bouncing on the bed,
Pachycephalosaurus fell off and broke his head.
Mama called the doctor and the doctor said,
"No more boneheads bouncing on the bed."

Nine little dinosaurs riding on a bike,
Stegosaurus crashed and smashed his spike.
The policeman yelled from atop his trike,
"No more nut-brains riding on a bike."

Eight little dinosaurs munching on a mooth,
Tyrannosaurus chomped and broke his tooth.
The dentist shouted from his dentist booth,
"No more sharp-tooths munching on a mooth."

 Seven little dinosaurs rafting down a river,
Spinosaurus flipped over and went all aquiver.
The lifeguard said, with a cold, wet shiver,
"No more silly-sails rafting down the river."

 Six little dinosaurs jumping off a peak,
Archaeopteryx dove and tweaked his beak.
One called the ranger and the ranger shrieked,
"No more feather-heads jumping off a peak!"

Five little dinosaurs playing in the street,
Ankylosaurus yelled, "A car to beat!"
He charged the street: squeal, screech, bleet, spleet,
No more dino-tanks playing in the street.

Four little dinosaurs acting sorta cool,
Supersaurus wore his shades to school.
The teacher sighed,
"Why that's against the rules."
No more super-lizards acting sorta cool.

Three little dinosaurs on a camp-out,
Chasmosaurus asked, "What's a lava tube about?"
He slid the tube, then blasted out the spout,
No more frill-seekers on a camp-out.

2 Two little dinosaurs watching baseball,
Saurolophus yelled, "Hey, that's a bad call!"
The umpire didn't like that talk at all,
No more big mouths watching baseball.

One little dinosaur walking all alone,
The sun burnt *Triceratops* into dried-up bones.
"Look," called the scientist, "at all these fossil stones."
No more three-horns walking all alone.

No more dinosaurs hanging on the brink,
They all disappeared in a geologic wink.
The doctor cried, "Well this just stinks!
Poor little dinosaurs all extinct."

ANKYLOSAURUS
(ANG-kil-o-SAWR-us)

Ankylosaurus had stout, bony plates all over its back. It was an armored tank, which made it very safe from attack.

ARCHAEOPTERYX
(ARK-i-op-ter-ix)

Archaeopteryx had wings and feathers, but probably was not a good flyer. It could do some flapping; however, its wings were weak, so Archaeopteryx used its wings to mainly soar and glide.

CHASMOSAURUS
(KAZ-mo-sawr-us)

Chasmosaurus had a huge frill that covered its neck and shoulders. The frill may have been used for display. The frill was far too fragile to provide defense against meat-eaters because it was only skin covering a bony frame.

PACHYCEPHALOSAURUS
(pak-ee-SEF-uh-lo-sawr-us)

Pachycephalosaurus is a member of a family of dinosaurs known as "bonehead." Boneheads had very thick skulls—about 10 inches (25.4 cm) thick, or about as thick as a ruler is long. Their brains were very tiny.

SAUROLOPHUS
(SAWR-o-LOAF-us)

Saurolophuses were duck-billed dinosaurs. They had nasal passages that amplified sounds they were able to make. Their loud honking was equally matched by their large mouths.

G L O S S A R Y